BEAK and WHISKER

Also by Jenny Nimmo
for young readers

Ill Will, Well Nell
Hot Dog, Cool Cat
Tatty Apple

Delilah and the Dogspell
Delilah and the Dishwasher Dogs
Delilah Alone

Jenny Nimmo

Illustrated by Ailie Busby

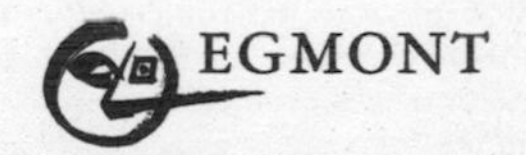

For Emily,

J.N.

To Mish,

with much love,

A.B.

First published in Great Britain in 2002
by Egmont Books Ltd
239 Kensington High Street, London W8 6SA

ISBN 0 7497 4854 0

10 9 8 7 6 5 4 3 2 1

A CIP catalogue record for this title is available from the British Library

Printed and bound in Great Britain by Cox & Wyman Ltd, Reading, Berkshire

Contents

1 Matthew and the Beast 1

2 Beak and Whisker 20

3 The Night of the full moon 39

4 Tansy and Beak 62

1 Matthew and the Beast

Tansy was afraid of birds. She knew it was silly, but she couldn't help it. 'Perhaps,' she said, 'when I was a baby, a bird flew into my pram and pecked me, or stole a toy.'

'No,' said Mrs Gray, Tansy's mum, 'Nothing like that ever happened.'

Tansy huddled deeper into the mound of bags on the back seat of the car. 'How d'you know it didn't happen?' she said. 'I could have been in the garden while you were indoors. So you wouldn't have seen it.'

'True,' her mum admitted, 'but it's unlikely. You'd have screamed.'

'You can't hear anything when the

vacuum cleaner's going,' Tansy muttered.

'*That's* true,' said Mr Gray. 'But whatever it is that makes you afraid of birds, you'll just have to get over it, Tansy. Because where we're going there'll be hundreds.'

'I know,' said Tansy sullenly. 'You told me.' She didn't mind the small birds, it was the large, dark birds she feared. The crows and rooks and jackdaws, birds that flocked together in a black cloud, cawing and shrieking.

Tansy's mum and dad had decided to change their lives. They gave up their work in the city and found something different in a country town.

They sold their flat in Station Road (where trains rumbled past all day) and bought half a house in the country, miles away from anywhere.

No one had asked Tansy what she wanted, but she told them anyway. 'I want to stay in Station Road,' she said, 'because I know everyone. I don't want to go somewhere strange and lonely.'

'You'll love it,' Dad said. 'You wait.'

And now, here they were, outside the new house, which looked very old, not new at all. It was a tall, grey-stone building with small windows and a very high chimney. On one side of the house strands of ivy hung over an upstairs window.

Tansy wondered which half of the

house was theirs. There were two front doors, two paths and two gardens separated by a thick hedge.

A boy came out of the house without the ivy.

Good, thought Tansy, I get the ivy.

'Oh, look, there's a boy next-door,' said Mrs Gray. 'He's about your age, Tansy. That's lucky.'

What's lucky? thought Tansy, boys are as bad as birds.

The boy had fair hair that flopped over his face, and he wore glasses. He clanged through the gate, came right up to the car and stared in at Tansy.

'Hullo!' He shouted as if she were miles away. 'I'm Matthew.'

'Oh,' mouthed Tansy.

Her dad climbed out of the car and shook Matthew's hand. Her mum did the same. Tansy stayed where she was.

'Come on, Tansy.' Mr Gray tapped on the window. 'Come and meet Matthew.' He opened the car door and Tansy reluctantly stepped out. Her dad said, 'This is Tansy. You'll be going to school together I expect.'

'Hi, Tansy!' said Matthew. 'I'm in Year Four. The bus stops right here. Are you coming to school tomorrow?'

'I . . .' Tansy began. She couldn't go on.

She heard her dad saying that she would be going to school by car on the first day, but after that she'd catch the bus with Matthew. And then Mr Gray saw Tansy's face.

'What's the matter, Tansy?' he said.

Tansy couldn't answer. She was staring at the roof. A shadow was settling over it; a chattering, cawing, murmuring cloud of birds.

'Birds,' whispered Tansy.

'Jackdaws,' said Matthew cheerfully. 'They live in the roof. We tried to get them out, but it's too late now; they've built their nests and laid their eggs. It wouldn't be fair.'

'It *isn't* fair,' said Tansy. 'It's not fair on me. I don't want to be here. I never did.' And she got back into the car and slammed the door.

The jackdaws were swooping in and out of the ivy, right above the window of the room that Tansy had decided would be hers.

Her mum and dad seemed very interested in Matthew. They ignored Tansy and began to pull things out of the boot. Matthew helped. They walked up to the new front door, Mum, Dad and Matthew, carrying bags and cases, and they all went into the new-old house.

Tansy stayed where she was, but after a moment she began to feel silly. So she got out of the car and walked through the gate. She took three steps up the path, and then it happened. Something dark floated through the air and landed on a plum tree, right beside her.

Tansy glanced quickly at the tree. A bird sat there, swaying on a branch. It had a feathery grey hood and bright, pearl-grey eyes. It turned its head and

stared at Tansy, and Tansy ran.

'Where are you?' Tansy cried, leaping through the front door.

'Here!' came Mum's voice.

Tansy tore down a dark passage towards the voice, and tumbled into a sunny kitchen.

Mum and Dad were filling the cupboards and Matthew was handing tins and packets of food to them. Tansy was annoyed to see the strange boy making himself at home in her new kitchen, but she kept quiet about it. She didn't mention the bird, either. She didn't want Matthew to laugh at her.

'I'm going to look at the rest of my new house,' she said. But at that moment the removal van turned up, and four large men in green overalls began to carry furniture into the house.

The passages and stairs in the house were very narrow, and it was quite a struggle to get everything in.

'Look out, Tansy! You'll get squashed,' yelled Dad as Tansy ducked behind a wardrobe.

'Tansy, you're in the way,' Mum shouted, as Tansy squeezed herself against the wall.

'You can come round to my house, if you like, while all this is going on,' said Matthew.

Tansy didn't want to go with Matthew, but she didn't want to get trampled to bits or squashed like a pancake, either, so she followed Matthew round to his side of the house. The bird, she noticed, had gone.

'This is Tansy,' said Matthew to his mum, who had just baked a cake.

Mrs Hood seemed to know who Tansy was. 'I was going to take this cake in to your mum,' she said. 'Moving house is a terrible business, isn't it?'

She offered Tansy a piece of cake.

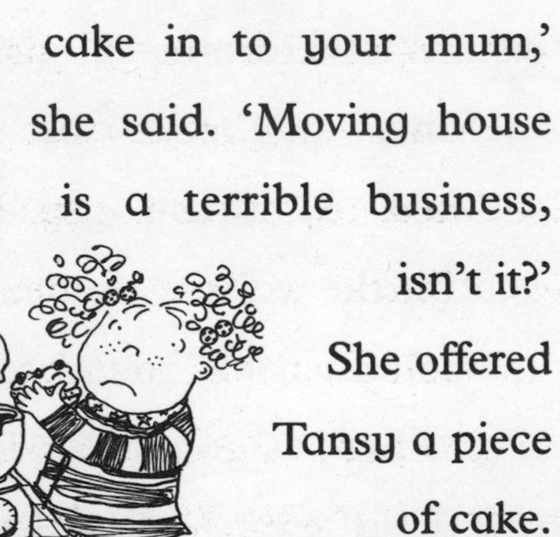

Tansy was starving. She took it, mumbling, 'Thanks.'

She'd barely taken two mouthfuls when Matthew said, 'Come and see my pets.'

Mrs Hood smiled. 'Go on Tansy. Don't worry about crumbs.'

Tansy followed Matthew into the back garden. He had two rabbits and four guinea pigs. They all lived together in a house a bit like a kennel. There was a long wire cage attached to it, almost as tall as Tansy. The rabbits were black and the guinea pigs were multicoloured. All the animals were out on the floor of the cage, nibbling: grass, carrots, a cabbage stalk, nuts and

seeds. It seemed to be their teatime, too.

At the end of the Hoods' back garden, a wall rose behind a bed of flowers. It ran all the way past the hedge and on into the garden next-door: Tansy's garden. Beyond the wall a green field sloped gently up to a row of trees. There wasn't another house in sight.

'It really is different,' murmured Tansy. She couldn't remember when she'd last seen a place without houses.

As she stared over the long stone wall, a huge ginger cat bounced on to it; as if from nowhere.

'Buzz off!' yelled Matthew. 'Go on. Go away!'

The big cat just glared at him.

'Don't shout at it,' said Tansy. 'It's only a cat.'

'It's the Beast,' said Matthew. 'Shove off!' he shouted at the cat again. 'We call him the Beast because he's fierce and cruel and greedy.'

'Where does he come from?'

'He used to live with an old lady in your house,' said Matthew. 'But when the old lady died, the Beast ran away. He's gone kind of wild. No one can catch him. He lives on mice and rats and things. I hate him. He even catches birds and eats them.'

Privately, Tansy thought this was no bad thing, but she realised Matthew was fond of birds.

Eventually the Beast ran off, but not before hissing at Matthew in a very loud and scary voice.

Time passed quickly in Matthew's garden. There were so many things to see: a pond full of goldfish, stick insects in a shed, newts with golden bellies and four white hens in a long pen. One of the hens had laid an egg in the nesting box, and Matthew pressed it, still warm and slightly damp, into Tansy's hand.

'Have it for breakfast,' he said.

And then Tansy's mum was calling her from the kitchen window, and Tansy said, 'Thanks for the egg. I'd better go now.'

'You can come round any time,' said Matthew. 'Come tomorrow.'

Tansy said, 'I'll think about it.'

When she got back to her side of the house, the removal men had gone, and Mum and Dad were in the living room, arranging the furniture. It looked strange in the new room.

'You seem to be getting on well with Matthew,' said Mrs Gray.

'Matthew's all right,' said Tansy, 'but he hates this big ginger cat because it's wild. He calls it the Beast. It used to

live here. This is its home. So I'm going to make it tame again.'

2 Beak and Whisker

Tansy's mum took her upstairs to look at the bedrooms. 'We thought you'd like this room,' said Mum, opening a door.

Tansy looked in. She saw ivy, prettily framing a window. Suddenly a bird, its wide wings dark against the sky, swooped up into the roof above the ivy. And Tansy heard the high-pitched shrieking of hungry baby birds.

'No,' said Tansy, 'Not this room.'

'But the other room's smaller, and this one has such a pretty window,' said Mrs Gray.

'I don't like it,' said Tansy. 'All that horrible squeaking in the roof. I'll never sleep.'

'Birds sleep too,' said Mum, 'and

soon the baby birds will grow up and fly away.'

'Please, Mum! I want the other room.'

Mrs Gray gave a big sigh. 'All right.'

Tansy's new bedroom was small, but it had advantages. She could look down into Matthew's garden. She could watch the rabbits and guinea pigs, and even make out the quick flash of the goldfish in the pond. She would be very happy in this room, she decided.

Next day Mrs Gray took Tansy to school. It was a very small school, not what Tansy was used to at all. But the teachers were helpful, and most of the children were friendly, especially a girl called Isobel.

Isobel was taller than Tansy. She had long fair hair, very straight and silky. Tansy had always wanted straight

hair. Isobel took Tansy's hand and showed her round. It was a bit confusing coming to a new school in the middle of the summer term, but Isobel made it easier.

Tansy didn't see much of Matthew. He was in her class but he spent most of his time with a boy called Mark.

At the end of school, Tansy's mum came to fetch her.

'How did it go?' asked Mrs Gray.

'OK,' said Tansy. 'There's a nice girl called Isobel.'

'Good,' said Mum. 'Would you like to go on the bus tomorrow?'

'Yes,' said Tansy. 'Isobel goes on the bus.'

When Tansy got home, she arranged her new school books on the bedroom windowsill. She was just putting the last book in place, when something caught her eye. The big ginger cat had jumped on to the garden wall. It crouched down with its paws tucked in and its tail flat on the stone.

Tansy ran downstairs. What would a cat like to eat? She took a small lump of cheese from the fridge.

'Where are you off to?' called Mrs Gray, as Tansy ran out of the kitchen.

'I'm going to feed the cat.'

She walked towards the wall. The ginger cat watched her. When she came close the cat began to growl.

'Stop complaining,' said Tansy. 'I've got some food for you.'

The big cat had an interesting face: a torn ear, a scratched nose, and one very long whisker sprouting from his eyebrow.

'Look out!' called a voice. 'The Beast will bite you!' It was Matthew, leaning out of his bedroom window.

'No, he won't,' said Tansy. 'He's just hungry.'

At that moment, the cat gave a hiss and a shriek. He stood and arched his back and spat at Tansy. Tansy dropped the cheese and ran back to the house.

'I don't think you're going to tame that cat,' said her mum. 'It's very fierce.'

The Beast had jumped off the wall and was biting into the cheese.

'I will,' said Tansy. 'You'll see.'

Next morning Tansy and Matthew got on the bus together. Isobel had saved Tansy a seat, and Matthew sat behind them.

'You shouldn't feed the Beast,' Matthew said, leaning over and breathing in Tansy's ear.

'He's not a beast. He's got a name.' Tansy leant away from Matthew. 'He's called Whisker.'

'Hunh!' Matthew sat back.

Tansy told Isobel about the cat. 'Poor cat,' said Isobel. 'It's sad he hasn't got a home of his own.'

'He will have – soon,' said Tansy.

Whisker didn't appear for several days, then, on Saturday when Tansy was helping her mum peg up the washing, there he was, looking rather the worse for wear. He sat on the wall, licking his paw and brushing

it over his torn ear.

'What can I give him, Mum?' asked Tansy.

'There's some fish left over from yesterday,' said Mrs Gray. 'I'm sure he'd like that.'

He did.

This time Tansy managed to get right up to the wall. When Whisker began to grumble and growl, she dropped the fish beside him and jumped back. Whisker seized the fish and ran off.

'It's working!' Tansy gave a jump of excitement. Then she looked round to see if Matthew had been watching. But he was nowhere to be seen.

On Sunday, Tansy stood by her window and watched Matthew clean out his animals. She wished she could help, but she wasn't sure if he was friendly any more, because of Whisker.

Her dad called her downstairs.

'Tansy, there's a funny noise outside the window. Can you hear it?'

Tansy could. It was a loud squawking noise. She had a very good idea what it was. 'No, I can't hear anything,' she muttered.

'I can.' Mrs Gray looked up from her paper. 'It sounds like a baby bird. Tansy, go and have a look.'

Tansy opened the front door and peeped out. A dark thing fluttered in the grass below the living-room window. High above, a jackdaw looked out of the ivy and called to its child.

The fluttering thing screeched. Tansy froze.

'Tansy, quick!' Matthew looked over the hedge. 'Do something.'

'You do it,' she said.

'You're nearer,' cried Matthew. 'Look out! The Beast will get it.'

And there was the Beast, Tansy's Whisker, creeping over the lawn towards the fluttering thing.

'TANSY!' yelled Matthew, racing to his gate.

Tansy almost jumped out of her socks. Before she knew what she was doing, she found herself hopping over the grass. Whisker

was about to pounce, but Tansy pounced first. She picked up the bony, shrieking creature and clasped it to her chest, while a growling Whisker glared up at her.

'Well done!' Matthew came running up to Tansy and reached for the bird.

'Ugh!' Tansy placed the struggling, half-feathered bundle into Matthew's hands.

A disgusted Whisker marched away from them.

'What are you going to do with it?'

Tansy asked Matthew.

'Well, the mother can't feed it down here,' he said. 'And if we put it back in the nest, it'll probably fall out again.'

'So you'll have to feed it.'

'Yes. I've done it before. Not with a baby jackdaw, though.' Matthew looked doubtful, which was unusual for him.

'Good luck,' said Tansy.

She went back indoors and told her parents.

'He's very good with animals, isn't he?' said Tansy's mum.

'Not cats,' said Tansy.

She tried to forget the baby bird, but she couldn't stop wondering how

Matthew was going to feed it. Perhaps it had died? That afternoon, curiosity got the better of Tansy. 'I'm going next-door to see Matthew,' she told her mum.

She went round and knocked on the Hoods' front door. Mrs Hood seemed to know why she had come. 'D'you want to see the bird?' she asked.

'I just wondered . . .'

'Come in,' Mrs Hood smiled. 'Matthew's just feeding it.'

As she went down the passage Tansy could hear a high-pitched squawking.

Matthew was in the kitchen, kneeling beside a small wicker shopping basket. He had what looked like a piece of

worm in his fingers. As Tansy peered into the basket, Matthew dropped whatever it was into a huge yellow beak. There was silence as the bird swallowed.

'I think it's had enough,' said Matthew.

'What did you give it?'

'Cut-up worm.'

'Uuurgh!' Tansy felt sick.

'Mum's going to get some tins of cat food,' Matthew told her. 'Jackdaws need meat you see, but only in tiny bits.'

'But to . . . to do what you did to a worm. That's disgusting.'

'It had to be done,' said Matthew. 'And I'll probably have to do it again.'

Tansy looked closer into the basket. The baby jackdaw had bright blue eyes. Its bony-looking wings were only partly feathered,

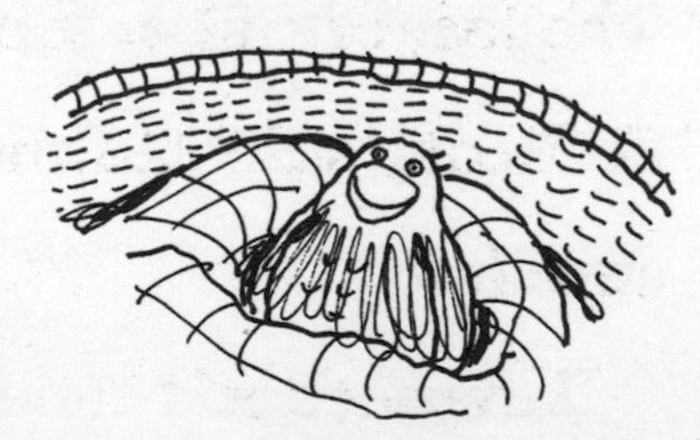

and the two halves of its beak were outlined in a fierce yellow. Even closed, the beak looked large. In fact the whole bundle looked big for a baby.

'I thought baby birds were tiny,' she murmured.

'Jackdaws are big birds,' said Matthew.

'How long are you going to feed it?'

'Until it can fly. That could take weeks. Its wings haven't grown yet. I'm going to call it Beak.'

'Beak?' exclaimed Tansy. 'You can't call it Beak. It should have a real name like Joe, or Bill or Jack.'

'Beak,' said Matthew firmly. 'It's my jackdaw.'

'I rescued it.'

Matthew went quiet. Tansy could see he wasn't going to change his mind.

'Tell you what,' Tansy said. 'If you call the Beast Whisker, I'll call the bird Beak.'

'Done!' said Matthew.

They shook hands. The baby jackdaw watched with bright blue eyes. And then it closed its silvery lids and fell asleep. Safe and full.

3 The night of the full moon

Tansy told Isobel about the bird. It was Monday morning and they were sitting on the bus. The cut-up worm wasn't mentioned. Tansy didn't think that would have been fair to Matthew.

'So what does it eat?' asked Isobel.

'Matthew's mum got some cat food,'

said Tansy.

Behind them, Matthew listened with a big grin on his face.

'Why don't you get some cat food for Whisker?' said Isobel.

Of course. Why hadn't Tansy thought of it? 'It's a great idea,' she said.

Matthew looked a bit worried when he got off the bus that afternoon.

Mrs Gray and Mrs Hood were chatting by the fence, as usual.

'I hope Mum remembered to feed Beak,' said Matthew. 'It's really important. He could die if he doesn't get enough food.'

Tansy hoped Mrs Hood didn't have to go and find worms. 'Does he wake up in the night?' she asked. Her mum had warned her that babies did this.

'Nope. He slept right through,' said Matthew proudly.

Tansy's mum suddenly held up a tin. 'I've got some cat food for Whisker,' she said.

'Mum, you're brilliant,' cried Tansy. 'I was going to ask.'

'D'you want to come and see Beak?' Matthew asked Tansy.

'Maybe. When I've fed Whisker.'

But Whisker didn't appear. Tansy spooned some cat food on to a saucer and put it on the wall. Then she waited. Waited and waited.

He's offended, thought Tansy. He wanted the baby bird and I wouldn't let him have it.

She decided not to go and see Beak. She wouldn't visit the jackdaw until she saw Whisker again.

Next morning the cat food had gone.

'He did come back, then,' said Tansy's mum. 'You just didn't see him.'

'It could have been another cat,' Dad pointed out. 'Or even a bird.'

'A jackdaw!' shrieked Tansy. 'A jackdaw stole Whisker's food!'

Mrs Gray told Tansy to calm down. They couldn't be certain.

Every day for a week, Tansy put a saucer of food on the garden wall. But Whisker never appeared. Tansy took the saucer in at night, in case a jackdaw got it.

On Saturday morning, Matthew looked over the hedge and asked Tansy why she hadn't been to see Beak.

'Because Whisker has disappeared,' said Tansy. 'I put some food out for him, but a jackdaw ate it.'

'Jackdaws don't eat cat food,' said Matthew. 'Not when they can get things that move: beetles and flies and moths and things.'

'Then why are you giving cat food to Beak?' asked Tansy.

'Because he can't catch his own food yet. And you wouldn't like me to spend my time cutting up worms, would you?'

'No,' Tansy agreed.

'Leave some food on the wall tonight,' said Matthew, 'and then keep watch. There's going to be a full moon.'

'There might not be.'

'Trust me,' said Matthew. 'I know these things. Got to go now. Come round tomorrow.'

'I'll think about it,' said Tansy.

There *was* a full moon that night. An orange moon. It appeared very early above the hill. And then it rose into the sky getting paler as the sky darkened. Tansy put the saucer of food on the wall before she went to bed. And then she watched from her bedroom window.

But she couldn't keep her eyes open. Her head sank back on to the pillow, and she fell asleep. When she woke up the moon was staring into her face.

Tansy knelt beside the window and looked out.

She'd caught him. There on the wall was the ginger cat, enjoying his meal.

Every night after that, Tansy put a saucer of food on the wall. Sometimes she saw Whisker, and sometimes she fell asleep before he arrived. But it gave her a good feeling to know that the wild cat's visits were becoming a habit.

He rarely appeared in daylight. Mrs Gray said he probably slept all day and worked at night. Cats were like that. They slept for eighteen hours out of twenty-four. Much longer than a human being.

Tansy began to visit Matthew. She told herself it was the rabbits she wanted to see, and the fat little guinea pigs. But she couldn't help taking a peep at the jackdaw. It was amazing how fast he had grown. Soon his wings were covered in sleek black feathers; his beak lost its fierce yellow and became slimmer and darker. He began to tumble out of his basket and flutter about, but still he couldn't fly.

Mrs Hood made Matthew find a bigger box and move Beak into the back porch. A young jackdaw was too messy for a kitchen. Matthew fixed a bamboo cane across the box and Beak would perch there, watching things. Whenever he saw Matthew, he would flap his wings excitedly and call for food.

Sometimes Matthew took Beak for a walk in the garden. Beak would sit on his arm, turning his head to stare at the ground, looking for insects.

And then Beak began to walk. He would stride across the garden, peering under stones, pecking at anything that moved. He was especially fond of woodlice. One hot Saturday, Matthew put a shallow dish of water on the lawn and Beak leapt into it. His two wings flew round like the sails of a windmill while water flew in all

directions. He looked so funny, Tansy couldn't stop laughing.

Of course it was rather risky, letting a non-flying jackdaw strut round a garden, but Matthew was always watching. And then, one day, he didn't.

Isobel had come to visit Tansy. They ate their tea outside, sitting on the stone steps that led down to the lawn. Tansy was just biting into a ham sandwich when Whisker appeared on the wall.

'It's your cat,' cried Isobel. 'Shall we feed it?'

'Don't scare him,' Tansy warned.

'We'll just walk up to him, really slowly, and put a sandwich on the wall.'

The two girls crept forward. Whisker watched them, but he didn't move. The girls reached the wall and Tansy slowly lifted her sandwich and placed it in front of Whisker. He didn't growl. He stared at Tansy suspiciously, then he bent his head to lick the sandwich. Tansy had been longing to touch him. Now was her chance. Her hand came up and she patted his back.

With a hiss and a spit, Whisker leapt away. He ran to the end of the wall and jumped down into Matthew's garden.

Horror of horrors! Tansy saw Beak strolling down the path. Whisker saw him too. He crouched, ready to spring.

Where was Matthew?

'Matthew! Matthew!' shrieked the girls.

The television was on in Matthew's house. He couldn't hear them. He was watching a programme about

robots, and the background music was very loud.

Whisker was in killing mode: belly on the ground, one paw moving very, very slowly, and then the other.

Tansy screamed, 'Go away!' She could hardly believe what she had said, but she had to do it. 'Go away!'

Isobel clapped her hands and shouted, 'Shoo! Shoo!'

Whisker took no notice. He was intent on his prey. The prey knew nothing about it. The prey couldn't fly. The prey didn't stand a chance.

Unless . . .

Suddenly, Beak looked up. He turned his head to one side and stared at Whisker, curious and then interested. The girls couldn't believe their eyes. Beak took a step towards Whisker.

Whisker couldn't believe it either. Small creatures usually ran away from him. He wasn't used to being stared at, and then approached. Whisker didn't know what to do.

At that moment Matthew appeared, 'Did somebody . . .?'

The girls pointed, frantic and silent. But Matthew had already seen Beak and Whisker. With a mighty yell, he rushed down the path.

Whisker leapt on to the wall and

over it. Beak walked into a flower-bed and peeped out. Still curious.

'How did that happen?' Matthew lifted Beak out of the flowers.

'It wasn't our fault,' said Tansy. 'Someone left your door open and Beak just walked out.'

'It was Mum. She's always forgetting.' He ran indoors.

Tansy wished and wished she hadn't shouted at Whisker. 'He won't trust me now,' she grumbled.

'What else could you do?' said Isobel. 'You were trying to save a bird's life.'

'Beak can take care of himself,' Tansy muttered. 'That's obvious.'

It was the last week of term. Everyone was talking about their summer holidays. But the Grays weren't having a holiday. 'We've moved house, that's enough excitement for one year,' said Mr Gray.

Tansy noticed that Matthew's rabbits and guinea pigs had gone. Their cage was empty. She saw Mr Hood and Matthew fixing a long pole across the cage. What was going on?

'Where are your rabbits?' Tansy called over the hedge.

Mr Hood was hammering.

'Come round and I'll tell you,' Matthew shouted. Beak looked up from his shoulder.

Tansy ran round to the Hoods' front door and Mrs Hood let her in. There were cases in the hall, neatly folded coats and a row of shoes.

'We're going to America on Saturday,' said Mrs Hood. 'A holiday of a lifetime. My sister lives there. But our cases don't seem to hold enough for five weeks.'

'Five weeks is a long time,' Tansy remarked.

'It is.' Mrs Hood looked very happy about it.

Mr Hood had finished his work on the cage. He looked very pleased with himself.

'What's happening?' asked Tansy.

'We're going to put Beak in here while we're on holiday,' said Matthew. 'He'll be safe, and he's got lots of room to flutter about, and even a place to sleep. He can perch on the pole Dad's fixed up.'

'Where are your rabbits?'

'Mark's looking after them.'

'Is he going to come and feed Beak?' asked Tansy.

'No, he can't do that. He lives too far away.'

'So who's . . .?' Tansy had a sinking feeling.

'You'll look after Beak, won't you?' said Matthew.

'Me?' cried Tansy. 'I can't. I can't look after a bird.

I'm not a bird person.'

'Yes, you are,' said Matthew. 'You just won't admit it.'

4 Tansy and Beak

'I'm a cat person, not a bird person,' wailed Tansy. 'I won't look after Beak, I won't.' She stood in the middle of the kitchen, grunting at her mum. 'How am I supposed to tame a cat, if I'm looking after a bird?'

'Calm down, Tansy. If you won't do

it, then I suppose I shall have to.' Her mum sighed. 'I promised to feed the chickens anyway. But we'll get a reward for that – new-laid eggs.'

Tansy calmed down. She felt mean. Her mum looked tired. 'All right, I'll do it,' she mumbled. 'I'd better go and find out *how* to do it.'

She went round to see Matthew again. He was kneeling beside Beak's new home looking rather glum.

'I don't think I want to go on holiday,' he said miserably. 'Something awful might happen to Beak.'

Tansy found herself saying, 'No it won't. I'll look after him.'

'Really?' Matthew looked more cheerful.

'Yes, really,' said Tansy, 'but you'd better show me how.'

Matthew explained things in rather a rush, and at first it sounded as though Tansy would be busy all day. The list of bird-chores was very long. There was

the bowl of water that had to be filled, the cat food that had to be minced up,

the crumbs and tiny bits of cheese that had to be scattered on the floor of the cage, and the hay in the nest that had to be changed once a week. 'And you'll have to scrub the perch now and again,' said Matthew. 'It gets a bit yucky.'

Tansy could have done without that last chore. 'Right,' she said, gritting her teeth. At least she wasn't going to have to cut up worms.

'He still likes to be fed by hand,' Matthew added wistfully. 'He gets a bit lonely.'

'Hm.' Tansy wasn't going to commit herself any further.

'Thanks, anyway,' said Matthew. 'We're leaving very early tomorrow, so in case you forget something, I'll write it all down and put the list through your letterbox.'

'Don't worry about a thing. You just go and have a good holiday.' Tansy skipped home, trying not to think about the problems tomorrow might bring.

By the time Tansy woke next morning, the Hoods had left. She looked out of the window. There was the cage, and there was Beak on his perch. Waiting. For her.

Downstairs she found the list Matthew had dropped through the letterbox.

'Now or never,' Tansy said to herself. She ran up to her room, dressed quickly and went round to the Hoods' back porch. The tins of cat food were stacked inside the door. An old spoon lay on top of the little tin bowl beside them. Tansy pulled back the ring on a tin marked 'Lamb' and spooned the meat into the bowl.

When she had minced up the cat food, she carried it down to the cage.

Beak saw her coming and he danced along the perch, flapping his wings excitedly. Tansy took a deep breath and opened the door. As she put the food in, Beak did something unexpected. He jumped on to Tansy's wrist. She froze.

'Mum! Mum!' squeaked Tansy.

Mrs Gray had just come in to the garden to feed the hens. 'What is it?'

'He's . . . he's on my hand,' said Tansy. 'Oooooo!'

'He won't hurt,' said her mum.

Beak took no notice of Tansy's squeaks. He perched comfortably on her wrist and pecked at the meat in the bowl.

Tansy dropped the bowl. A surprise for Beak. He turned his head

questioningly, and then dropped down to eat the spilt food. He also tried to lift the bowl. Tansy withdrew her hand and bolted the door quickly.

Later on she scattered crumbs through the wire at the top of the cage. That wasn't so risky. Now and again, throughout the day, Tansy would hear Beak calling: a sad and rather demanding squawk. But she tried not to hear the birdcalls. Her job was to feed and clean. Nobody said anything about making friends.

There had been no sign of Whisker since Tansy shooed him away. But she still put cat food on the wall at night, and something was eating it. Cat, bird, squirrel or rat? Nobody really knew.

For the next few days Tansy followed Matthew's list very carefully. She got used to Beak hopping on to her hand, and, although she wouldn't admit it, Beak's excited greeting rather pleased her. She was beginning to feel a bit lonely. Isobel was on holiday too, and the village was far away.

On Friday evening, Mr Gray said, 'We're

going to the seaside tomorrow!'

'Really!' cried Tansy. 'For a holiday?'

'Just for the day,' said her dad. 'I think we all deserve a treat, don't you?'

Tansy remembered Beak. What should she do about feeding him?

'Put a day's supply of food in his cage,' Mum said. 'I'm sure he'll be all right. He's a big bird now.'

So, on Saturday morning, Tansy put a large bowl of cat food in the corner of Beak's cage. She scattered crumbs on the floor as well. Beak watched her inquisitively. Tansy noticed that his round blue eyes were changing colour. Gradually they were turning pearly grey.

'Goodbye,' said Tansy. 'We're off to the seaside.'

It was the best day she'd had for ages. The sun was hot and the beach was perfect. Tansy spent all her time running in and out of the sea, fishing for shrimps and building sandcastles. Now and then she

poured water over her mum and dad, to keep them cool.

It was still light when they got home, but very late. Tansy went round to see Beak. He wasn't on his perch. He wasn't near his bowl of food which was half full. Tansy began to panic. Where was Beak?

She saw a dark form in a corner. Tansy crawled into the cage and

touched it. She felt soft, warm feathers, but there was no movement. Gently, she lifted the bird off the ground. Beak's silky lids were half-closed, and his head lolled forward.

'Oh, Beak, what is it?' Tansy whispered. 'What's the matter?'

And then she noticed that the water bowl was empty. She had forgotten to water, and it was at the top of Matthew's list.

'I'm sorry, I'm sorry,' Tansy sobbed.

'Tansy, what are you doing?' Mrs Gray peered into the cage.

'Oh, Mum, I think Beak's dying.'

Tears rolled down Tansy's cheeks. 'I forgot the water, and it was so hot today.'

'Bring him inside,' said Mrs Gray.

Carefully cradling the bird, Tansy crawled out of the cage and followed her mother into their kitchen.

Mrs Gray wet a finger and held a drop of water close to the bird's black beak. He gave a faint cheep. She tried again and he opened his beak. Next she held out a spoonful of water, and this time Beak sipped

for himself, putting his head back and letting the water trickle down his throat.

'Mum,' breathed Tansy. 'You've done it. You've saved him.'

'Let's try some food,' said Mum.

Beak pecked a few bits of foods from Mrs Gray's hand, and then he half-closed his eyes. Slowly, he moved along Tansy's arm. When he reached the crook of her elbow, he tucked his head into her sleeve, and Tansy could almost feel a tiny sigh escape from him, before he fell asleep. The top of his head was crowned with tiniest of black feathers.

Tansy hardly dared to move. She sat in the kitchen with Beak tucked into her

arm as if he belonged there, and only when she was sure that he was sleeping peacefully, not ill or dead, Tansy laid him gently into the nest of hay at the back of his cage. Perhaps it wasn't just water that he had needed. Perhaps, he had been lonely.

Next morning Beak woke Tansy with his usual chirpy calls for food. This time Tansy brought him right out of the cage. She walked round the garden while he perched on her arm. She sat on the stone steps and he ran on to the lawn, picking at ants, woodlice, beetles and flies. Tansy kept an eye on the wall. Just in case Whisker decided to appear.

'If only you could fly, you'd be safe,' Tansy told the bird.

She'd noticed that the other young jackdaws had begun to fly. They would flutter out of the ivy and follow their parents into the trees, chattering with excitement. They were very noisy birds.

Beak had no one to teach him how to fly. 'It'll have to be me,' said Tansy. 'Otherwise you'll never learn.'

She picked him up and when he'd settled on her wrist, she swung her arm, very gently. Beak took off, his wings flapping wildly. Then he plummeted to the ground.

Every day after that, Tansy took Beak for a flying lesson, and every day he managed to flutter a little further. And then, one bright afternoon, he flew

right down the garden and landed on the roof of the chicken shed.

'Well done,' said Tansy, with a tiny pang of sadness.

Beak flew on, into the trees where his brothers and sisters were calling.

At teatime Tansy was quite tearful. When Mum asked her why she was upset, Tansy said, 'Beak can fly.'

‘That’s wonderful,’ said Mrs Gray. ‘Matthew will be impressed.’

Beak was a flyer now. He wouldn’t go back into the cage, but he still came to Tansy for food. She didn’t know where he slept. Perhaps he sat in the trees with his head tucked under his wing, or nestling among the other jackdaws. But wherever he went, he always came back in the morning, shouting for breakfast.

Sometimes he would land on Tansy’s shoulder, and sometimes on her head. And she found that she wasn’t afraid of dark wings swooping any more.

One day Beak didn’t come back.

'He will,' said Tansy's mum. 'You'll see.'

But two days passed and there was no sign of him. Only a week to go and Matthew would be home. How was Tansy going to explain?

'Beak can fly. He's free. He's happy,' said Mrs Gray. 'Matthew will be glad for him.'

'No, he won't,' said Tansy. 'He'd want to be the one who let Beak go. He'd want to say goodbye.'

She walked round the garden, calling Beak's name and making frantic jackdaw sounds. But the flocks of chattering birds that flew overhead took no notice.

Tansy was looking into the sky when she almost tripped over a furry mound by the wall. Whisker had returned. Tansy had been leaving his food out every night, but she'd givenup watching for him. Now, here he was, fast asleep, at her feet.

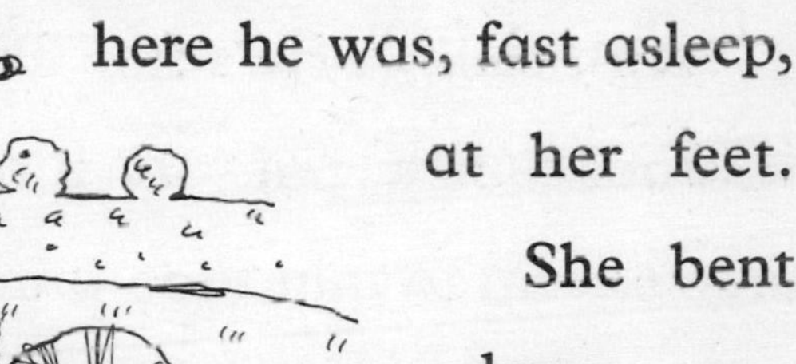

She bent down, very slowly, and touched the cat's head. Whisker opened his eyes. He didn't growl. He didn't run away.

'Wait there,' Tansy said softly. She ran indoors and spooned some cat food into a saucer.

‘Has Beak come back?’ asked her mum.

‘No. It’s Whisker.’ Tansy carried the saucer down to the bottom of the garden. Whisker hadn’t moved. But when the food arrived he sat up and ate it, very noisily. And when Tansy risked another quick pat on his head, he didn’t seem to mind too much.

In three days, Whisker has taken his first nervous steps back into his old home. In four days, Tansy was stroking him. On the fifth day, he purred. At the end of the week he spent the night in a cosy box in the Grays’ back porch.

Beak had left, but Whisker had returned to take his place. If a nasty

little suspicion crossed Tansy's mind, she banished it, instantly.

The day that Tansy had been dreading arrived. The Hoods came back from their holiday. They drove up on a drizzly morning, and Matthew immediately rushed out into the garden. Tansy watched from her window. She saw Matthew peer into the empty cage. And then he began to call her.

'Tansy! Tansy, where's Beak?' He looked up at the window, and it was too late for Tansy to hide.

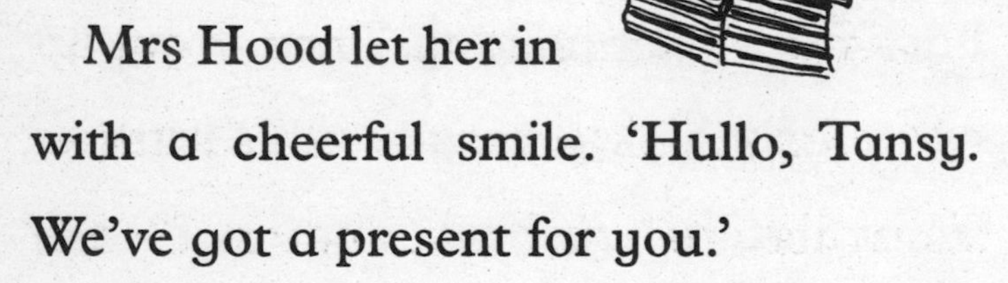

Dragging her feet, not knowing how she could explain, Tansy went round to Matthew's house.

Mrs Hood let her in with a cheerful smile. 'Hullo, Tansy. We've got a present for you.'

'Thanks,' Tansy smiled back. 'I've got to see Matthew,' she said, 'about the bird.' She made her way though the house and out into the garden.

'Where's Beak?' Matthew demanded.

Tansy explained, as best she could, about the flying lessons. 'I'm sorry you weren't here to say goodbye to him,' she said.

Matthew looked suspicious. And then something unfortunate happened. Whisker appeared and rubbed his head against Tansy's leg.

'What's he doing here?' said Matthew.

'Whisker's tame again. Isn't it good.'

'No, it's not good,' said Matthew, his voice rising. 'He's eaten Beak, hasn't he?'

'No! No!'

'Yes, he has. And you know it!'

'I don't. He wouldn't.' But Tansy

couldn't be sure, that was the trouble.

'He's a beast, that cat, and he always will be!'

'It's not true,' said Tansy, fighting back the tears.

'Don't lie. Don't you ever . . .' Matthew's mouth suddenly dropped open. He looked really peculiar.

Tansy was hardly aware of the soft touch in her hair, as she sobbed, 'I couldn't keep Beak in a cage, could I? Not when he could fly?'

Matthew just stared at her head.

Tansy put up her hand and felt two

twig-like legs. Beak stepped on to her wrist. Gently, she brought the bird down and held him out to Matthew.

'Tansy you *are* a bird person!' he said

And Tansy had to agree.